THE Monstore

WRITTEN BY
TARA LAZAR

ILLUSTRATED BY
JAMES BURKS

ALADDIN   NEW YORK   LONDON   TORONTO   SYDNEY   NEW DELHI

for
SALE

$

For Alan, Elianna, and Autumn —T.L.

For my mom and dad —J.B.

ALADDIN

An imprint of Simon & Schuster Children's Publishing Division   1230 Avenue of the Americas, New York, NY 10020   First Aladdin hardcover edition June 2013   Text copyright © 2013 by Tara Lazar

Illustrations copyright © 2013 by James Burks   All rights reserved, including the right of reproduction in whole or in part in any form.   ALADDIN is a trademark of Simon & Schuster, Inc.,

and related logo is a registered trademark of Simon & Schuster, Inc.   For information about special discounts for bulk purchases, please contact Simon & Schuster Special

Sales at 1-866-506-1949 or business@simonandschuster.com.   The Simon & Schuster Speakers Bureau can bring authors to your live event. For more information or to

book an event contact the Simon & Schuster Speakers Bureau at 1-866-248-3049 or visit our website at www.simonspeakers.com.   Designed by Karin Paprocki

The text of this book was set in ITC Novarese Standard.   Manufactured in China   0313 SCP   10 9 8 7 6 5 4 3 2 1   Library of Congress Cataloging-

in-Publication Data   Lazar, Tara.   The Monstore / by Tara Lazar ; illustrated by James Burks. — 1st Aladdin hardcover ed. p. cm.

Summary: Zack's house is overrun when he buys defective monsters from the Monstore.   ISBN 978-1-4424-2017-5 (hardcover) /

ISBN 978-1-4424-4648-9 (ebook)   [1. Monsters—Fiction. 2. Brothers and sisters—Fiction.] I. Burks, James, ill.

II. Title.   PZ7.L4478Mo 2013   [E]—dc21   2010044846

At the back of Frankensweet's Candy Shoppe, under the last box of sour gum balls, there's a trapdoor.

Knock five times fast, hand over a bag of squirmy worms, and you can crawl inside . . .

THE MONSTORE.

The Monstore sells only the most useful monsters, just right for doing tricky things around the house.

SALE

MANAGER

1/2 off

The kind that love crab-leg casserole.

The kind that glow in the dark.

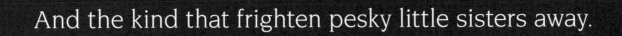

And the kind that frighten pesky little sisters away.

Except Manfred the monster.

He was supposed to stop Gracie from snooping
around in Zack's bedroom.

Instead, Manfred showed Gracie his favorite hiding place.

Zack wanted a refund.

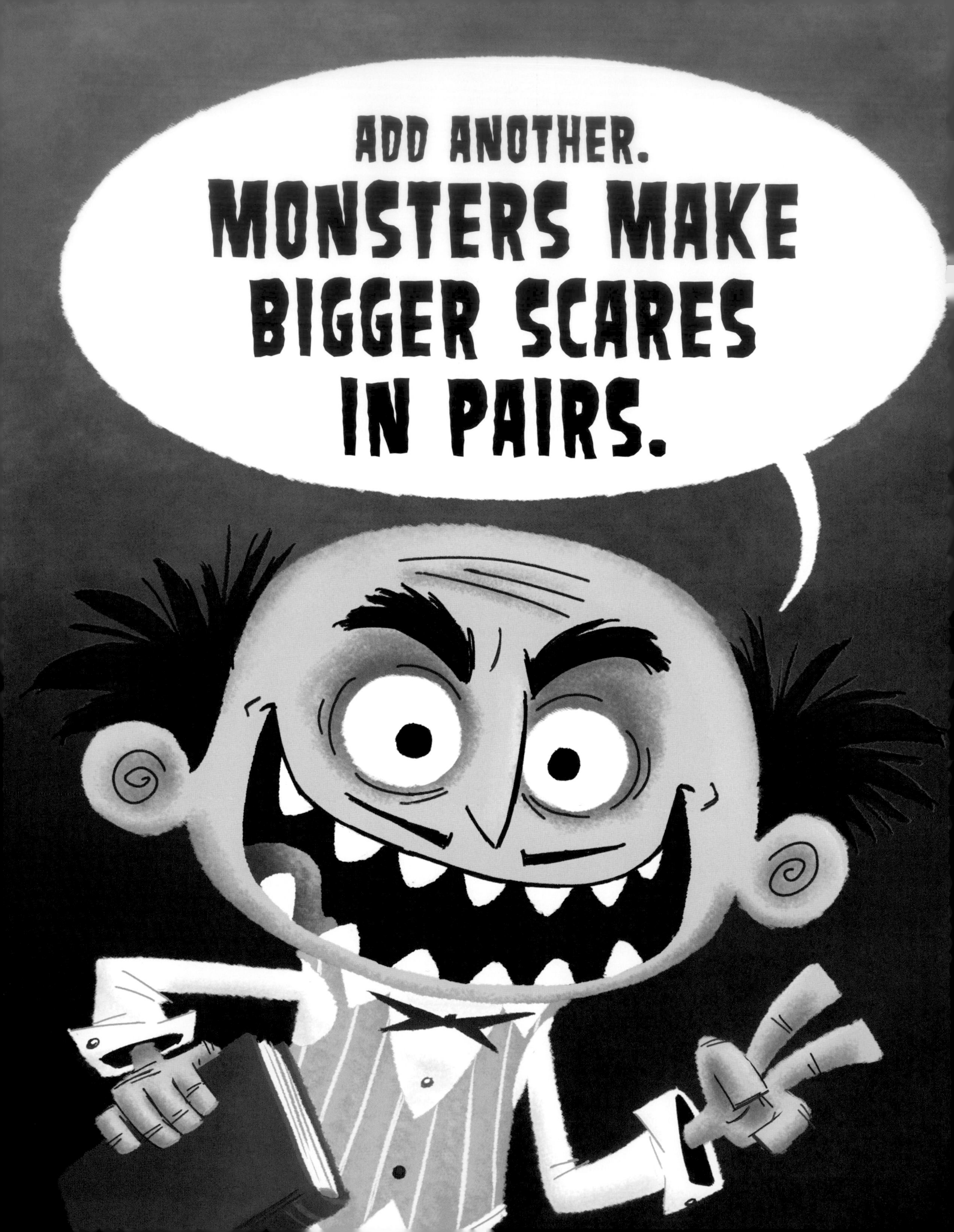
ADD ANOTHER.
MONSTERS MAKE BIGGER SCARES IN PAIRS.

So Zack brought Mookie home.

He was supposed to stay up into the wee hours and keep Gracie

from sleepwalking into Zack's bedroom.

Instead, Manfred and Mookie taught Gracie a new way to wake him up.

Zack had the right to a refund.

ADD ANOTHER.
A MONSTER THREESOME IS MORE GRUESOME
THAN A TWOSOME.

So Zack brought Mojo home.

He was supposed to set booby traps around Zack's bedroom, capture Gracie, and haul her away. No more sneaky sister snooping, sleepwalking, or snatching his stuff.

Instead, Manfred, Mookie, and Mojo threw Gracie a monstrous birthday bash right there in his room.

That was it!

Zack begged, whined, grumbled, and collapsed onto the cash register. But the Monstore manager just pointed to the sign:

I DESERVE A COMPLETE AND TOTAL REFUND!

NO RETURNS
NO EXCHANGES
NO EXCEPTIONS

So Zack kept buying . . .

and trying . . . and buying . . .

Pretty soon Zack had collected so many monsters
he had to pack up and move to the basement.

In the middle of the night, the splintery stairs made a creepy

CREAK.

Finally the monsters were working! Zack sprinted up the stairs two at a time to see what monsterly mischief had spooked his little sister.

Zack was tempted to leave that glitzy, glittery thing right there, but Gracie was right. It was pretty hideous. That monstrosity had more spikes than crab-leg casserole.

Slowly and carefully, Zack rid the room of the tiara terror.

YOU'RE THE BEST BROTHER EVER!

After that, Gracie and the monsters cleaned up the party decorations fiendishly fast.

And then Gracie and the monsters marched out of Zack's room.

Finally the bedroom belonged to Zack again. . . .

. . . and the monsters belonged to Gracie.

All of them.

Every single one.

An entire mob of monsters!

NO
RETURNS
NO
EXCHANGES
NO
EXCEPTIONS

When Gracie got home,
she smooshed the monsters
back inside.

WHAT ARE WE GOING TO DO?

Gracie smiled. She had a monster of an idea.

So now . . . at the back of their crooked old bike shed, under a box of rusty roller skates, there's a trapdoor. Knock five times fast, hand over a bag of squirmy worms, and you can crawl inside . . . **THE MONSTORE 2**.

Just remember: No returns. No exchanges.